Clara Vulliamy

KT-479-193

THE PAW PRINT PUZZLE

# Dotty
# DETECTIVE

HarperCollins *Children's Books*

First published in Great Britain by HarperCollins
*Children's Books* in 2016
HarperCollins *Children's Books*
is a division of HarperCollins*Publishers* Ltd,
1 London Bridge Street, London, SE1 9GF

The HarperCollins website address is: www.harpercollins.co.uk

11

Text and illustrations © Clara Vulliamy 2016

ISBN 978-0-00-813245-3

Printed and bound by CPI Group (UK) Ltd, Croydon, CR0 4YY

MIX
Paper from
responsible sources
FSC® C007454

FSC™ is a non-profit international organisation established to promote
the responsible management of the world's forests. Products carrying the
FSC label are independently certified to assure consumers that they come
from forests that are managed to meet the social, economic and
ecological needs of present and future generations,
and other controlled sources.

Find out more about HarperCollins and the environment at
**www.harpercollins.co.uk/green**

for Mark,
with all my
love x

# Read the whole series:

- *Dotty Detective*
- *Dotty Detective and the Pawprint Puzzle*

**This book
belongs to...**

# DOT

*and McClusky*

**FRIDAY**

This is me – Dot! And TOP DOG
McClusky!

With our best pal Beans...

...we are the JOIN THE DOTS DETECTIVES.

There is no mystery that we cannot get to the bottom of. We have even solved one *FIENDISHLY TRICKY* case already!

Me and Beans are in the same class at school.

Nobody knows about our detective work – we are extra-super-outstandingly brilliant at keeping it **TOP SECRET.**

Here are our special badges.

We wear them under our coat collars
so we do not BLOW OUR COVER.

Right now, I'm here in what nearly everyone thinks is just my bedroom. But really it is the

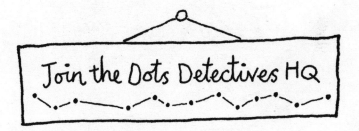

Join the Dots Detectives HQ

Ta-da! A GRAND TOUR of all my favourite things!

Here is all my stuff...

my stamp set

*and my notebooks*

*and my special pens*

*and my code books*

*and my stickers –*
*there is actually no such*
*thing as too many stickers.*

12

*(I am a HUGE stationery fan.)*

*Oh and DOTS! I have dots literally \*everywhere\* in my room.*

*And here are my* **FRED FANTASTIC - ACE DETECTIVE** *books...*

Me and Beans both love **FRED FANTASTIC.** *It's the best TV show EVER. Fred is a detective who solves dastardly crimes by finding clues and piecing them together, just the same as we do. Mysteries are like huge complicated puzzles.*

*I LOVE puzzles. The trickier the better.*

*In fact, I'm going to do an extra-difficult spot the difference to relax before I go to sleep.*

# SPOT THE DIFFERENCE

# Saturday

Having Choco Crispies for my breakfast.

The twins (my brother and sister Alf and Maisy) are super-noisy about who gets the toy in the cereal box but I hardly notice because I'm loving the milk in my bowl going all chocolately. SLURP.

OOPS! spilled some! ➘

Mum says we haven't been on an outing for AGES, which is true. I bet she'll suggest the swings.

But she looks in her purse and then she says, "We are going to Westbury Farm Park and we are going RIGHT NOW!"

WOO HOOOOO!

I ♡ the Farm Park *so* much.

The twins are going crazy and cheering, although I'm not sure they even remember what the Farm Park is.

They try to take their pyjamas off and run around the room at the same time, which is bound to end in **DISASTER.**

Luckily, I am **super-skilled** at calming them down.

Bundling into the car. I say, "Don't worry, McClusky – YOU are going on a brilliant outing too!"

We drop McClusky off at Grandpa George's house. "Come on McClusky, we're off to the allotment!" says Grandpa George.

McClusky barks happily. I wonder if he remembers that there are dog biscuits kept specially for him in the potting shed?

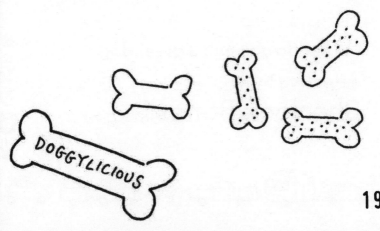

DOGGYLICIOUS

The journey is taking FOREVER.
SO MUCH TRAFFIC! *sigh*

"Are we nearly there yet? Are we
nearly there yet? Are we nearly there
yet?" the twins are asking every five
seconds.

But I distract them with some of my
very cheesiest jokes.

**"What do you call a great dog
detective?
Sherlock Bones!"**

"Why did the girl put peanut butter all over the road?
**To go with the traffic jam!**"

"How do you make an octopus laugh?
**With ten-tickles!**"

Then the twins make up their own, which aren't jokes at all...

"Why did the chicken cross the road?
**Potato!**"

They collapse into hysterical giggles and even though it's not funny I can't help laughing too.

Mum says who needs an animal park with a carload of monkeys like us?

But AT LAST we come around the corner... and we've arrived!

Riding on a tractor!

22

Jumping on the hay bales!

Feeding baby goats with a
bottle – they tug so hard I
can only just hold on!!!

Funny photo of me pretending to
*hold up a cow*!!

And now this is my BEST BIT.

Me and the twins sit in a circle with some other children and are given really small animals to gently hold and stroke.

We get to meet a chick!

SO SOFT...

And a black and white rabbit:

And a guinea pig who never stops talking...

*burble burble squeak squeak !*

Aawww

Going back to the car now. The twins carry the picnic basket, which is nice as they aren't usually the most helpful people in the universe.

Back home and heading to my room.

Walking down the hallway just as it's getting dark... and I have the oddest feeling that someone is behind me.

But when I turn around **there's** nobody there.

**STRANGE!**

 *It's nearly bedtime. I'm just sorting out my things and putting my hair-slides into rainbow colour order, when I hear a NOISE just outside my room.*

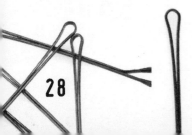

# Tap-tappit

## Tap-tappit...

*I pop my head around the door but the hallway is empty.*

*MYSTERIOUS.*

# SUNDAY

Something is odd and different at breakfast. It takes me a minute to realise what it is... the twins are really quiet. And then they ask Mum for a blanket.

"Are you two coming down with a cold?" she asks and feels their foreheads. "We will have a nice quiet day at home today."

Mum and I make some cookies and decorate them with dots of coloured icing.

I give McClusky only a VERY tiny bit.

The twins are whispering to each other in their secret twinny language, then they hurry to their room.

They are definitely acting strangely today!

So I'm watching **THE WIZARD OF OZ**
with Mum. I'm wearing my

# sparkly red SHOES

especially, and we have hot chocolate
in our Dorothy mugs.

It is probably the nine hundredth time we have seen it, which isn't NEARLY enough for us!

McClusky barks whenever Toto appears. McClusky is a **massive** Toto fan.

Think I'll head to my room and get ready for school tomorrow.

In the hallway I feel something soft brush against my leg, but by the time I turn on the light there's nothing there.

# SPOOKY.

 *It's bedtime and I'm nearly asleep, when... **what's that??***

*There's a NOISE outside my door, but different this time.*

Light footsteps scurry past, then a door bangs shut.

I hop out of bed and peep around the door but again the hallway is completely empty.

The twins must be fast asleep by now, McClusky is in his bed in the kitchen, and I can hear Mum on the phone in her room, so it can't be her.

This is getting to be VERY MYSTERIOUS. Who – OR WHAT – is

making these strange noises in the hallway?

What IS going on???
There's only one thing for it...

it's a case for the Join the Dots Detectives!

ON THE CASE

*Clues so far are:*

❓ ❓ ❓ ❓ ❓

CREEPY atmosphere in the hallway
SPooKY feeling against my leg
STRANGE noises in the night

❓ ❓ ❓ ❓

*I write a message to Beans, using my*
*INVISIBLE INK KIT!*

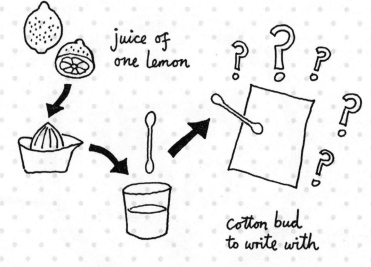

juice of
one lemon

cotton bud
to write with

*I write the message on a piece of paper and leave it to dry.*

*The wet writing completely vanishes...*

*...but tomorrow when Beans holds it up against a light that is warm but not TOO hot, the message will magically appear!!!*

# MONDAY

I am leaving my secret message
in the chink in the wall next to the
school gate, mine and Beans' usual
hiding place. Then I hurry to line up.

I see Beans rush over to the wall.

On the way to assembly, I spy Beans
take a detour to the light in the
corridor, and when he sits down in

the hall he gives me a WOAH!!! face.

Assembly is Mrs Bagshott telling us about INSPIRATIONAL WORDS OF THE WEEK.

This week they are

AIMING

HIGH.

Fiyaz mimes throwing an imaginary football up high towards the portrait of our school founder and pretends it bops him right on the nose.

"Nobody thinks that is funny, Fiyaz,"
says Mrs Bagshott, even though
everybody is laughing.

Mrs Bagshott is our head teacher.
Even in high heels she is really short.

Breaktime. With Beans in the
Lookout – our special place in the
playground where we keep an eye on
things and talk detective.

He gets out the note...

> THERE IS SOMETHING SPOOKY GOING ON IN MY FLAT !!

I tell him about the clues so far.

"COOL!" says Beans. "Remember the
**FRED FANTASTIC** episode last week,
*The Case of the Ghastly Ghost*? The
first signs were spooky noises and

a feeling that somebody was there even though they couldn't see them... your flat might be HAUNTED!"

"I don't believe in that stuff. I've never seen a ghost," I say. "But it is VERY creepy."

"I've never seen a ghost either," says Beans, "although my Auntie Celia saw one in a shop once, wafting about near the pickled onions."

"Well SOMETHING is going on," I say, "and it is up to the Join the Dots

Detectives to get to the bottom of it!"

Back in the classroom, our teacher Mr Dickens does a little dance and tells us that he has NEWS! Mr D always makes us giggle.

"Next Monday," he says, "it is our class's turn to do the assembly! Our theme will be SPACE."

Hooray! I think space is ACE. It is SO HUGE and most of it we still don't know anything about. If you think about it, it's actually the

biggest mystery of all.

But you know where you are with science because it is all about FACTS.

I know a cool space fact: it's impossible for astronauts to eat toast because there is no gravity. The crumbs detach themselves and float about in the spacecraft!

At lunch, Beans is giving me lots of top tips about ghost-hunting. He seems to know FABULOADS about the supernatural.

"Look out for COLD SPOTS," he says, "places that are extra chilly for no reason.

"AND objects moving around even if no one has touched them," he goes on, "because then you might have a POLTERGEIST!"

"But we need to be scientific and find the evidence – one way or the other!" I say.

Beans is more super-certain about the ghost explanation than I am. But if he has a feeling about this we need to **FOLLOW THAT HUNCH!** as **FRED FANTASTIC** always says.

I still don't really believe my flat is haunted, but a good detective keeps an open mind and investigates ALL the possibilities.

Annoyingly, Laura Drew – who is BAD NEWS – has been listening.

"OOOOOH, do you live in a haunted house, Dot?" she says.

"I heard about a girl once who saw a ghost and she was so terrified her eyeballs popped right out on springs... and then her head actually fell off and rolled away!"

I don't answer.

Back home, we are having broccoli cheese but with no cheese because Mum forgot to buy any, so basically broccoli.

I eat it super-speedily. In a hurry to INVESTIGATE.

In the hallway, I cannot feel any cold spots. There IS a damp spot underfoot, but to be honest in this place that could be *anything*.

As for objects on the move, it is

seriously chaos everywhere in our flat – a whole army of poltergeists could be living here!

*I am REALLY trying not to think about what Laura said. I know she is deliberately trying to frighten me.*

*Even though I don't believe in ghosts, I still find them quite scary.*

*So to distract myself I find my glow-in-the-dark dotty stickers, and make them into constellations on my wall. When I turn out the light they look*

*COOL BANANAS as* **FRED FANTASTIC**
*would say.*

*At bedtime I listen out for strange noises. It's all quiet tonight.*

*I am DETERMINED not to be scared.*

# Tuesday

Pouring with rain today. Thank goodness for my spotty raincoat and matching umbrella.

Having school lunch with Beans. We are really excited because today I am going to his house after school.

"We could make more gadgets for our Join the Dots Detectives kit!" says Beans.

Beans has already made a periscope that was VITAL in figuring out our last case.

I am EXTRA-excited now.

I open my lunchbox. Mum has

accidentally put in a ball of string instead of my apple.

In English we are writing poems about Laika the space dog, the first animal to orbit the earth. Mr D tells us there is a sad ending.

I would NEVER let McClusky go into space without me.

We are all SO SAD about Laika that Mr D says, "Hmmm. I know..."

He gets a packet of Oreos from his desk and shows us how you can cut away some of the icing inside to show the different phases of the moon!

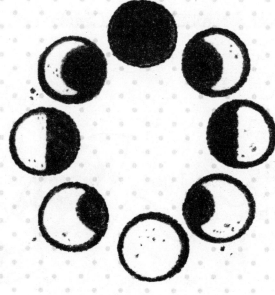

Mr D shares out the moons afterwards, and even though we only get a crumb each they are DELICIOUS.

Then we watch a video of astronauts playing ping pong in space with special bats and a droplet of water instead of a ball. AMAZING!

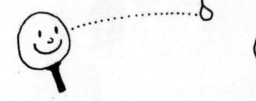

After school, I go back with Beans to his house.

At tea, we are squashed up at one end of the kitchen table.

This is because Beans and his dad are drawing a complicated map together, on the back of a long roll of wallpaper, which takes up lots of room.

They do a bit more on it each day, just for fun. It looks brilliant!

His dad gives us tinned peaches for our pudding, which we think is *THE CAT'S PYJAMAS* as **FRED FANTASTIC** would say.

After tea, it's time for gadget-making. Beans gets his shoebox of treasures and tips it out on to his desk.

**WOW**, I feel like I'm in **The Wonderful World of Beans** Museum!

"I have a BRILLIANT idea!" says
Beans. "Rear-view glasses!"
Beans is SO CLEVER.

This is how we make the rear-view
glasses...

two pairs of old sunglasses

four pieces of mirror card...

glued on the inside,

and here

here

glue

"Now I can see what's behind me without turning round!" I say. "Perfect for spying vital clues in THE CASE OF THE SPOOKY NOISES!"

Then we watch **FRED FANTASTIC - ACE DETECTIVE**. We think Fred Fantastic's golden rules for solving a mystery are really useful.

 **STAY FROSTY. Always be on the lookout.**

 **FOLLOW THAT HUNCH! If you've got a funny**

feeling, you may be on to
something important.

 **USE YOUR NOODLE.
Think!**

 **A LIGHT-BULB MOMENT.
A sudden genius idea.**

 **GET PROOF. You MUST
have the evidence before
you can solve your case.**

Fred says sometimes you need to use
your SIXTH SENSE too, to see things

that other people can't.

He also says **JEEPERS CREEPERS – USE YOUR PEEPERS!** Even when you are scared stiff, keep going and trust in what you see with your own eyes!

In tonight's episode, Fred's cool sidekick Flo is kidnapped and Fred needs a speedboat, a ball of wool and a string of sausages to rescue her.

When Mum picks me up to go home, I make sure I have my new rear-view glasses safely in my pocket. "STAY FROSTY, DOT!" whispers Beans.

Chatting with Mum while we walk back. She shows me a hole in her glove. "Nibbled!" she says. "It must have been that naughty McClusky!"

That's strange. McClusky doesn't normally nibble clothes.

Back at home, when no one is looking, I put on my special glasses.

I go along the hallway and into each of the rooms, but I don't see anything unusual.

But **FRED FANTASTIC** never gives up on a case. There's definitely something STRANGE going on, and I'm going to keep super-sleuthing until I find out what it is.

# WEDNESDAY

McClusky is acting weird this morning. He refuses to walk with us to school – usually he is first to the front door, DESPERATE to go out!

"No time to argue about this, McClusky!" says Mum. We leave him at home.

On the way to school Mum says we are having a special tea party on Sunday because it's her birthday.

Grandpa George and my aunts and cousins are all invited, and we will make a huge chocolate cake because it's Mum's favourite.

I offer to help. I have spectacular skills, especially in the bowl-licking department.

Today in class we are working on our space assembly. Some of us will be in the solar system. Me and Amy are

PLUTO!

Pluto is cute

Mr D tells us that Pluto is so far from earth, that trying to see it is like trying to see a walnut that is thirty miles away. "Smaller than a dot, Dot!" he says.

Laura is Jupiter. "MY planet is thousands of times bigger than YOUR planet," she says.

But I don't care. I think Pluto is MUCH cuter!

In art, we make costumes for Joe and Nadia who are going to be Yuri Gagarin and Valentina Tereshkova –

the first man and the first woman in space.

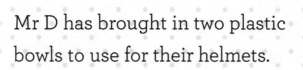

Mr D has brought in two plastic bowls to use for their helmets.

Our PE lesson is gymnastics. We are practising our sequences.

I am in a pair with Frankie Logan. He is a whirling dervish – all over the place, but KEEN.

"Fancy footwork, Frankie!" says Mr D.

In the afternoon, Laura is talking about her starring role in the class assembly with her friends. But I hardly notice because I'm really really busy.

Me and Beans are playing TEACHER BINGO. We each write down three words that Mr D says a lot and we cross them off when he says them.

Whoever crosses off their three words first, wins.

Beans is winning with **BRILL** and **SUPER-DUPER**...

But I catch up with **FAB** and **AMAZEBALLS**...

I WIN WITH **COOLIO!**

Walking home, Mum tells me that McClusky is in the dog house today. He doesn't actually have a dog house of his own...

It means he's in big trouble for bad behaviour. "He's been growling and barking at everyone who visits!" says Mum. "I hope he behaves himself on Sunday."

Back at home I find McClusky sitting in the hallway outside the broom cupboard, being very growly.

His untidy hair is sticking up even more than usual.

At tea, the twins are saying, "Mmmm, salad, can we have LOTS of salad, please!" Which is very strange, because they usually avoid lettuce like the plague and hide the cucumber in their socks.

Today EVERYBODY is acting weird!

*I'm in my room, making a paper-clip chain. It helps me think.*

*I'm wondering about McClusky.*

*Why is he growly in the hallway? What IS going on with him?*

grrr..... grrrrr......

*I make a list of all the things it could be...*

McClusky is...

CROSS because he ~~wants~~ to watch the ~~Wizard of~~ Oz more often ?

SAD because I only ~~gave him~~ a tiny bit ~~of cookie~~ with coloured icing ?

SCARED because ...

*Of course, I suddenly see – IT'S ANOTHER CLUE in* **THE CASE OF THE SPOOKY NOISES!**

*I write a new note to Beans using the invisible ink. Then I go to bed.*

*In the night – there's that noise again!*

Tap-tappit

Tap-tappit...

*...and a sort of clicking...*

*I put my head under the covers and I close my eyes tightly.*

**This time** *I do feel A BIT scared.*

*I don't think I believe in ghosts, but what else could it be???*

# Thursday

The twins say they have tummy aches and need to stay at home.

By the time Mum has persuaded them out of the front door we are in a HUGE RUSH to get to school on time.

Into the school playground and – oh no! It's 'Wear A Hat For Charity Day' and we have forgotten!!!

Me and Mum quickly look in our bags.

She has three pink bus tickets and an envelope with interesting stamps on it.

I have some spotty tape and a few paper clips.

In less than two minutes...

...my hat is looking pretty good!

I only *just* have time to leave my secret message in the chink for Beans...

But we don't have time to talk about it in registration because Mr D has **AN IMPORTANT ANNOUNCEMENT.**

One of the plastic bowls for the helmets is missing!

We all hunt for it EVERYWHERE… but only find Kirstie's lucky wind-up false teeth ("Hooray!" says Kirstie) and Frankie Logan's old lunchbox, which has a very strange smell coming from inside it.

I am just opening my mouth to speak to Beans about the message… but then it's maths and we all move to our separate tables. I sit at the table with tricky extra tasks, which I really like.

I make an excited **WE URGENTLY NEED TO TALK!** face across the room to Beans. He makes an impatient **YES WE DO!** face back.

Walking over to the ICT suite, to research our solar system facts.

We have to dodge a puddle of rainwater in the corridor. Mr Meades the caretaker is sighing and mopping it up.

AT LAST we look at the message...

MCCLUSKY HAS SIXTH SENSE — HE HAS SEEN SOMETHING IN THE HALL !!!

"Of course! Animals have a nose for the supernatural," says Beans.

"But it's not enough to have SIXTH SENSE – we need to be scientific and **GET PROOF**," I say. "It's Fred Fantastic's biggest Golden Rule for solving a case."

Beans is coming round to my house after school. This is our BEST chance to get the final clues so we know for absolute certain: ghost or no ghost...

Fingers crossed we get A LUCKY BREAK.

In art, we make planets out of balloons and tissue paper.

WOW, Kirstie has nearly finished her Saturn AND its rings! Our Pluto is basically still a small gluey lump.

Laura makes

WOOO~WOOOOO

ghost noises when she walks behind my chair. It startles me. I am feeling very jumpy.

When we get to my house, the first thing we find is McClusky still sitting outside the broom cupboard in a growly mood.

He has even dragged his bed there!

"He hasn't budged all day," says Mum. "Not even for a Doggylicious biscuit bone, which is his absolute favourite! He growls at everyone who goes past.

"I hope he doesn't spoil the tea party on Sunday," she says, looking worried. "Maybe I will have to cancel."

Me and Beans sit down on the floor next to him. "What is it, McClusky? Tell us what you see!" He doesn't answer. Obviously.

The twins are lurking about nearby. They seem to be listening intently.

But Beans has another GENIUS PLAN. Dusting for footprints!

"Ghosts don't leave footprints," says Beans, "so if we only find footprints belonging to you, your mum, the twins or McClusky, that will PROVE it's a ghost!"

We need:

a soft brush from my artbox

a tin of cocoa powder

We sprinkle the powder over a patch of wooden floor in the hallway and brush it gently so it covers the area evenly. Footprints start appearing!

I sketch the different footprints we see...

Quick! I get the dustpan and brush and clear up before Mum finds us covering the house in chocolatey dust.

 *We hurry to HQ to examine the evidence.*

this big shoe must be Mum

this looks like MY shoe ⟶

small one could
be Maisy or Alf →

these pawprints must
be McClusky's

Nothing – and NOBODY – else.

 We think about the clues:

- Noises in the night.
- Creepy feeling in the hallway.
- No footprints.

- *Animals are spooked by the supernatural, which is why McClusky is being so strange...*
- *Maybe the twins can sense it too, which explains why they have been so odd lately?*

# HOLY MOLY!

*"It MUST be a ghost – it has to be!" I say.*

*"Floating above the ground, leaving no footprints!" says Beans.*

*Up until now I didn't think I believed in*

*ghosts, but what else could it be?*

*And if the ghost carries on driving McClusky crazy, Mum will cancel her birthday tea party!* **DISASTER!!**

*At bedtime, Mum comes in to say goodnight. She says, "Is there something on your mind, Dot? I can practically SEE the cogs whirring inside your head!"*

*How can I explain to Mum – she will think I'm as crazy as McClusky!*

*But one thing's for sure...*

*I MUST GET RID OF THE GHOST BEFORE MUM'S BIRTHDAY TEA!!!*

## Friday

Raining AGAIN.

"Just some celery for breakfast please, Mum," say the twins.

WEIRDER AND WEIRDER!

No more lemons to write a secret message to Beans. I have nothing new to say right now anyway, but a good detective should always be prepared.

Mum is looking inside the fruit and veg box and saying, "How **odd!** It's practically empty!"

But I do find one last single banana down at the bottom.

This gives me an idea. I take a cocktail stick from the kitchen drawer and put it in my lunchbox with the banana.

In class Mr D says, "I am down in the dumps today because now BOTH plastic bowls that we need for our assembly costumes have disappeared!"

"It is a **CALAMITY**," he says. "Today is our last day to prepare!"

We are all really worried about our assembly.

Joe and Nadia were going to perform a moonwalk – but astronauts without helmets? It's just not possible! Will their bit have to be cancelled?

First Mum's birthday tea, and now
the assembly moonwalk – everything
is just going from bad to WORSE!

"Where could the bowls possibly be?"
me and Beans are wondering.
But that's not our only worry.

At lunch I take the banana and the
toothpick out of my lunchbox and
secretly get to work, under the table
so no one can see.

Nothing shows at first:

But after a few minutes I say, "You dropped your banana, Beans."

He looks totally mystified, but I give him a meaningful intense stare and he takes the banana and looks at it.

HOW DO YOU GET RID OF A GHOST???

But Beans only knows about finding ghosts – not how to make them go away!

"I have lost the ball in the long grass, Beans," I say. **FRED FANTASTIC** says this a lot.

This has nothing to do with an actual ball and overgrown plants. It means you feel totally lost and don't know what to do next.

Beans says he feels just the same. We have absolutely **NO IDEA** how to get rid of the ghost before Sunday.

Laura sidles up to us. "Will your house be haunted *forever*, Dot?" she says. "Is it tormenting you and driving you out of your wits?"

"I read about a family once who heard ghostly screams," she goes on, "and they were so petrified they literally turned into four

## wobbly jellies."

I don't say anything. I don't trust my
voice not to shake.

In PHSE we are doing 'It's good
to be me!'. We each tell the class
something that we have achieved
that we are proud of.

Kirstie is pleased that she scored the
winning goal in football this week.

Marcus says that he moved a snail
from the middle of the pavement so it
didn't get trodden on.

Laura has so many things to tell us that Mr D has to interrupt and say, "Moving on now, Laura, thank you."

I'm not really in the mood for this today.

 **"USE YOUR NOODLE**, *DOT!" I say to myself at bedtime, as I'm getting into bed. If we don't get rid of the ghost, McClusky will RUIN Mum's birthday tea party!*

*I remember the chapter about ghosts in my* **FRED FANTASTIC – CRAZY**

**CRIME CAPERS** *book, so I get it down from the bookshelf.*

*Fred is investigating a haunted hotel. He uses his* sixth sense *to try to see the ghost, but when he looks closely it turns out to be the hotel owner's arch-enemy wearing a sheet to scare away the guests.*

*This doesn't help me at all.*

## SATURDAY

Mum takes me and the twins to Pink Vanilla for a milkshake! It is my NUMBER ONE favourite place.

I have a Snickerdoodle Shake, with ice cream, cinnamon and hundreds and thousands.

I manage to forget about the ball in the long grass for a bit.

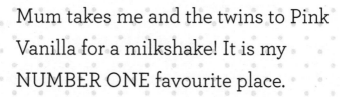

MMMM...

Back at home, McClusky is pacing up and down in the hallway, growling at everyone as they go past.

It all comes flooding back. The tea party is tomorrow!!!!!!

"That dog is driving me crazy! I really think I WILL have to cancel," says Mum. The chocolate cake is already made. She looks VERY disappointed.

Time is whooshing past *super-horribly-quickly* and now it's evening.

Watching the rain on the window. I haven't done a single thing to get rid of our spooky visitor and I'm running out of time!

On my way to bed, I feel it again – I am SO SURE there is someone else here...

McClusky is still lurking about outside the broom cupboard. He gives me a strange look. I'm certain he knows more than he can tell me!

*I wake up. A noise! This time RIGHT OUTSIDE my door.*

DOT HQ

Tap-tappit

Tap-tappit...

# CLICK CLICK...

*and a sort of...*

# SQUEAK!!!

*THIS time, I AM scared half out of my wits. But I am going to send this ghost packing ONCE AND FOR ALL. A birthday tea party is at stake!!!*

*So I get out of bed, tip-toe to the door and peep outside.*

In the dark I can just make out McClusky standing outside the broom cupboard, almost as if he is guarding it.

I start to think...

Was it his pawsteps I heard?

I think about the pawprints we dusted...

I look at my sketches of them again.

These are definitely McClusky's, but these ones...???

*I remember the* **FRED FANTASTIC** *haunted hotel story.*

*I realise what it is I have to do. Even when you're spooked:*

**JEEPERS CREEPERS, USE YOUR PEEPERS!**

*And as I creep out into the hallway, I think about the twins being weird this week, super-helpful carrying the picnic basket, suddenly super-keen on salad...*

*And Mum's nibbled glove...*

*And then all of a sudden I have*

## A LIGHT-BULB MOMENT!!

*I think I've got it!!!!*

*I rush to the broom cupboard, throw open the door...*

...and there, cuddled up in a blanket in amongst the mops and cloths and buckets... IS A BLACK AND WHITE RABBIT!!!!!!!!!

McClusky rushes past me into the cupboard... to chase the rabbit?

But no! He curls up close to it instead, very protectively.

Now Mum is here, and the twins have woken up and they are here too. We slowly put the pieces together.

The twins smuggled the rabbit home from Westbury Farm Park in the picnic basket, and have been looking after it all this time.

McClusky has stood guard, **PROTECTING** his new friend.

The twins are jumping up and down talking ten to the dozen both at the same time, and I can't understand a word of it.

Mum is looking astonished and cross.

"So THIS is why my fruit and veg box is empty!" says Mum.

Then Mum says, "Well that's enough drama for one night. We will sort this out in the morning." She finds an empty cardboard box and puts the rabbit cosily inside it.

I quietly close the broom cupboard door and give McClusky a hug. Poor McClusky – in the dog house, just because he was trying to do the right thing!

To think that THIS was my ghost all along!

But even better than that, Mum's birthday tea party is saved!

# Sunday

Grandpa George comes over to look
after us so that Mum can drive down
to Westbury Farm Park to take the
rabbit back.

Mum tells the twins that it was wrong
and the rabbit wasn't theirs to take,
but she could see they had done a
jolly good job looking after it.

The twins say a sad goodbye to the rabbit and give it a special card they have made, as well as the last bit of carrot they had been saving. More of a stump really. And they've had it a few days, so it is a bit bendy!

As Mum picks up the box with the rabbit inside, she looks at me,

the twins and McClusky, and says,
"Honestly, you crazy crew – you
drive me

But as she goes out of the front door,
I see she is slightly laughing to
herself.

Being extra nice to the twins. We
play indoor camping behind the sofa.
They soon cheer up.

Having extra hugs and a chat with McClusky, and giving him TWO Doggylicious biscuit bones.

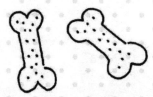

I hope he's not missing his rabbity friend, but he's still got me I tell him. He gives me a lick as if to say, "You're my BEST friend."

When Mum gets back we have less than THREE MINUTES to lay the table for the tea party and put up the birthday bunting...

...before the doorbell rings and the first guests arrive!

**MONDAY**

Lining up to go into school, I tell Beans all about how the ghost wasn't a ghost at all but a rabbit from Westbury Farm Park. He is absolutely amazed!

I say, "The pawprint-dusting worked BRILLIANTLY! The rabbit's pawprints were the most important clue, we just didn't see it at the time."

Beans says, "YES!"

Then he says, "It's a pity the rear-view glasses weren't more useful, though."

We both get out our pair and put them on.

We walk over to our classroom. It's our class assembly and we mustn't be late.

"HEY! LOOK!" says Beans.

We peer into our rear-view mirrors, gasp at what we see and turn around.

There, up on a high ledge in the corridor, are the two missing plastic bowls, half full with water!

It turns out that Mr Meades put them there to catch the rainwater under a leak in the roof. He didn't know they were important.

We tell Mr D and he is OVER 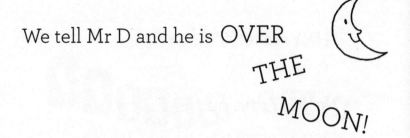 THE MOON!

Joe and Nadia are in the assembly after all! They quickly get into their astronaut costumes WITH helmets and they look **ACE**.

Laura makes a ghostly

**wooo~ wooooo**

noise again as we go past and starts
to say "I heard about a ghost once
who..."

But we make toothy rabbity faces,
and long ears with our hands, and
burst out laughing.

Mr D tells Mrs Bagshott that me and
Beans saved the day.

"Well done, you two!" she says. "As a reward you can choose the next Inspirational Words of the Week." After a speedy whispered discussion, we choose –

## USE YOUR PEEPERS!

Fred Fantastic would be proud of us!

Now I must grab my Pluto and rush over to the hall for assembly.

Another case...

But what will our next dastardly
difficult mystery be?

# Have you read?

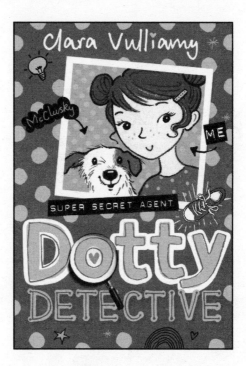

When someone seems set on sabotaging the school show, Dot is determined to find out how, and save the day!

Join Dot, Beans and McClusky
on their next case...

LOOK OUT FOR ANOTHER

coming soon...